MICHAEL DAHL PRESENTS

SIDE-SPLITTING STORIES

ATTACK OF THE DEADLY DIAPERS

By Megan Atwood

Illustrated by Ethen Beavers

STONE ARCH BOOKS
a capstone imprint

Michael Dahl Presents is published by Stone Arch Books,
an imprint of Capstone.
1710 Roe Crest Drive
North Mankato, Minnesota 56003
www.capstonepub.com

Library of Congress Cataloging-in-Publication Data
Names: Atwood, Megan, author. | Beavers, Ethen, illustrator.
Title: Attack of the deadly diapers / by Megan Atwood ; illustrated by
  Ethen Beavers.
Description: North Mankato, MN : Stone Arch Books, [2020] | Series: Michael
  Dahl presents: Side-splitting stories | Audience: Ages 8-12. | Audience:
  Grades 4-6. | Summary: Ten-year-old Angie DelMar is sure that there is
  something creepy and dangerous about her new neighbor, Ms. Doody:
  somebody who has a book entitled The ABCs of World Domination is
  obviously up to no good; but when Angie and her friends steal the growth
  serum intended to create giant insects they accidentally release it at
  the local day care—and the town is suddenly besieged by giant screaming
  toddlers in diapers.
Identifiers: LCCN 2019039621 (print) | LCCN 2019039622 (ebook) | ISBN
  9781496587053 (hardcover) | ISBN 9781496592095 (paperback) | ISBN
  9781496587107 (eBook pdf)
Subjects: LCSH: Toddlers—Juvenile fiction. | Eccentrics and
  eccentricities—Juvenile fiction. | Inventions—Juvenile fiction. | Best
  friends—Juvenile fiction. | Humorous stories. | CYAC:
  Toddlers—Fiction. | Size—Fiction. | Eccentrics and
  eccentricities—Fiction. | Inventions—Fiction. | Best friends—Fiction.
  | Friendship—Fiction. | Humorous stories. | LCGFT: Humorous fiction.
Classification: LCC PZ7.A8952 At 2020 (print) | LCC PZ7.A8952 (ebook) |
  DDC 813.6 [Fic]—dc23
LC record available at https://lccn.loc.gov/2019039621
LC ebook record available at https://lccn.loc.gov/2019039622

Designer: Hilary Wacholz

Printed and bound in the United States of America.
PA100

MICHAEL
DAHL
PRESENTS

Michael Dahl has written about werewolves, magicians, and superheroes. He loves funny books, scary books, and mysterious books. Every Michael Dahl Presents book is chosen by Michael himself and written by an author he loves. The books are about favorite subjects like monster aliens, haunted houses, farting pigs, or magical powers that go haywire. **Read on!**

TABLE OF CONTENTS

A "LAFFY" LAUGH!

When I was in middle school, my friends recorded me laughing. (They did it in secret.) I guess my laugh sounded so goofy that it made them laugh too. My friends were pretty funny themselves. They told great jokes and hilarious stories. I wish I had written them down. But that gave me the idea to have some of my new friends write down their stories. If you feel a chuckle or a guffaw deep inside while reading, let it out. Who knows—maybe your laugh will end up in a video!

Michael Dahl

CHAPTER 1

A NEW NEIGHBOR IS ALL THE BUZZ

Angie DelMar held the curtain and stared out the window at the older lady moving in next door. She'd hoped it would be someone who was ten—her age—or around that age, anyway. Instead, it looked like her new neighbor was a boring grown-up. Summer would be a snoozefest.

Her best friend, Cooper Sanchez, droned on as she looked. "But anyway, the day care people said that Chloe and Cara are two now, so they need to stop taking off their diapers. . . ."

Angie nodded but then squinted harder as she gazed out the window. Her curly red hair got in her face, so she brushed it aside. She whistled through the gap in her two front teeth.

". . . because people have *stepped* on the diapers and gotten poo—"

"Cooper," Angie said, "what does that box say?"

Cooper climbed up on the couch next to her. "It says, *DO NOT TOUCH—DANGEROUS*," he said. "Did you hear anything I just said?"

Angie nodded. "Sure. Diapers. Day care. Twin sisters. I got it." She flipped around and put her tongue between her teeth. "I think there's something weird about our new neighbor."

Cooper sighed. "You never listen to me."

"Huh? Did you say something? Never mind: let's go meet our new neighbor," Angie said. She grinned her biggest grin—the one she thought could talk Cooper into anything. They'd been best friends and neighbors since they were babies. She'd learned all the tricks to trick him—or rather, *encourage* him—into doing things with her.

"Uh . . . let's wait until she's done moving. And until our parents make us," Cooper said, frowning.

"Let's be proactive," she said. It was her mom's favorite word. She didn't know exactly what it meant, only that her mom said it to her deputies when she wanted them to do something they didn't want to do. As the town's sheriff, Angie's mom got to tell people what to do a lot. Angie liked doing that too.

Cooper frowned deeper. "I really don't think—"

"Great! Let's go!" Angie said. She grabbed Cooper by the hand, dragging him out the door.

They ran across the yards, Angie huffing just a little. The lady had disappeared inside the house, though the door was open as movers kept moving boxes.

When they reached the door, Cooper tugged at Angie. "Let's go back."

But Angie wasn't listening. She peered into the house and saw a door all the way at the back. A sign read, *MOVERS, DO NOT COME IN HERE UNDER ANY CIRCUMSTANCES.*

A mystery. She grinned and elbowed Cooper. "Look at that door," she whispered.

Cooper stood on his toes, and then his eyes widened. "Don't even think—"

"You're right! We should check it out!" Angie

said. A mover was coming up the front stairs.
Angie got out of the way and then followed him
into the house.

The mover turned to go up the stairs, and
Angie walked to the mysterious door. She put
her ear next to it. A strange buzzing sound came
through. She turned around to wave Cooper in
but stopped short.

Her new neighbor stood right in front of her.
"What are you doing, girlie?" said the woman.
She smiled the creepiest smile Angie had ever
seen.

Angie swallowed. "We . . . uh . . . I came to
meet you! I'm your neighbor," she said.

The lady frowned. "Kids, huh?" She shuddered
a little. She took Angie's upper arm and walked
her to the front door. "You should stay out of
people's houses, little lady," she said.

Cooper stood by the front door, eyes still wide. "H-hello," he said. "I'm Cooper. This is Angie."

The lady eyed him. "Another kid? This town is crawling with them," she said under her breath. "Well, I'm Ms. Doody."

Angie felt her eyes widen, and she laughed. "Ha! Ms. Doody!" But the expression on the lady's face made Angie stop laughing. She swallowed. "Oh. You weren't kidding."

"No, I wasn't, girlie. My name is Ms. Doody"— Angie couldn't help laughing again—"and this is my house you're trespassing in." She pushed Angie out the door so she was standing by Cooper.

Cooper pointed to the book in Ms. Doody's hand. "I like to read too. What is it you're reading?"

Angie squinted to see the title. Ms. Doody hugged the book closer to her and said, "None of

your beeswax, little man. Now, time to go home." Then she shut the door right in their faces.

They turned around and started walking slowly down the front steps. Cooper whispered, "Did you see the title of that book?"

Angie nodded. "Oh yeah. And I think we had better get into that secret room. Anyone who carries around a book called *ABCs of World Domination* is up to no good!"

CHAPTER 2

SNEAK-A-BOO

"It's just . . . I *know* my yogurt would be perfect for the day care," Cooper's mom said. She sat beside Angie's mom on the living room couch. "Kids love the stuff! And you know, the day care is a national chain. But Mika, Chloe and Cara's day care teacher, won't sit down with me. And I made *so* much yogurt, Beth. So much. It's just sitting in a refrigerator in my garage." She threw her hands up. "But she won't talk with me about it. I think she thinks I'm a fool."

Angie loved it when Cooper's mom came over to talk to hers. They got wrapped up in conversation for *hours*. Angie had no idea what the yogurt talk was about, but she wasn't really listening. She was plotting a way to get back into Ms. Doody's house.

She yelled to her mom in one long string of words, "We're going out to play and Genevieve is meeting us!"

Her mom yelled back, "Okay, stay close!" Then she kept right on talking to Cooper's mom.

Cooper followed Angie outside and crossed his arms. "You asked Genevieve to come over?" Genevieve was their mutual friend. Kind of. She was really more Angie's friend.

Angie ignored him.

Cooper said, "Did you invite Genevieve over so it would be two against one?" Just as he said that, their other, older neighbor Harvey walked up. Harvey was two grades ahead of Angie and Cooper, but he still liked to hang out with them. Angie thought he was annoying. But Cooper always made her be nice.

"What are you up to this fine day?" Harvey asked. Angie rolled her eyes, and Cooper elbowed her. Harvey always sounded like he was a million years old when he spoke.

"Nothing—" Angie said.

"Want to play?" Cooper said at the same time.

Harvey said, "I'm too old to 'play,' but I will spend time with you, if you so wish."

Genevieve walked up. "Hey, guys. Hi, Harvey! What's up? You said there was an emergency, Angie. I'm here!"

Cooper glared at Angie, but she pretended she didn't see. "Our new neighbor is trying to take over the world," she said. "We need to get into her house."

Genevieve blinked twice. Then, in her cheery way, she said, "Okay!"

Cooper huffed, and Harvey said, "I highly doubt that an adult would—"

"I have an idea," Angie said, ignoring everyone. She pointed to some squirt guns sitting in a pile on the border between her and her neighbor's yard. "Harvey and Genevieve, you play squirt guns and distract Ms. Doody—"

Genevieve snorted. Loud. "Did you say Ms. Doody?"

Cooper and Angie snickered. "Yeah," Angie said.

Harvey looked at them. "Ms. Doody? As in—"

"Yep," Angie said. "Ms. Doody." All of them giggled. Then Angie continued, "So you and Harvey will distract Ms. Doody"—they all giggled again—"while Cooper and I look in the window where the secret room is."

"I don't like it," said Cooper.

"Fun!" said Genevieve.

"What is 'squirt guns'?" Harvey said.

"Great! Let's go. I think Ms. Doody"—everyone giggled—"is in her side yard. Coop and I will run around to the window while you guys squirt at each other by her. She'll yell at you—she hates kids."

Cooper said, "Wait—"

"Okay, go!" Angie said. Genevieve and Harvey

ran to the squirt guns. Angie grabbed Cooper's hand and dragged him to the back window.

When they reached the window, they ducked down underneath it. Then they both slowly stood up to look through the glass.

But to Angie's disappointment, the shades to the window were drawn. She kicked herself for not thinking of that.

Cooper said, huffing, "If you would *listen* to me, Angie, I would have said she probably had the shades closed!"

Just then she heard a garbled yell. Genevieve and Harvey came racing around the house. Gen was grinning madly, but Harvey looked confused. "Why did you squirt that lady, Genevieve?" he asked.

"Yes, why, Genevieve?" drawled Ms. Doody. She stood on one side of the house, her hair

dripping. She saw Angie and Cooper, and her eyes narrowed. "YOU," she said. "Here you are again, trespassing!"

Angie stood taller. "What do you have in that secret room?" she said, sticking her chin up.

Ms. Doody grinned a not-nice grin. She took out her phone, dialed a number, and spoke into it. "Yes, sheriff. I have some little trespassers here I'd like removed. I'm at 219 Leahy Street. I believe the trespassers' names are Cooper and Angie?"

Angie groaned. Cooper sagged next to her. And in less than a second, she heard her mom bellow, "ANGIE ROBERTA DELMAR, GET OVER HERE!" She looked slowly toward her house and saw her mom and Cooper's mom standing at the front door, hands on their hips.

Angie turned to confront Ms. Doody, but she was gone. She heard a swift *shhuuush* and saw movement in the window. Ms. Doody had opened the shades and now waved at them gleefully. She turned to the side and swept her arm around the room.

There was nothing there. A desk, a lamp, and a laptop were the only things in the room. It was empty.

Cooper glared at Angie and stomped away toward his mom. Angie turned away from Ms. Doody's mean grin and walked slowly back to her own house.

Genevieve ran up to her and put her arm through Angie's. "It was worth a shot, Angie. Should I text you later?"

Angie sighed. "Make it two days. I'm definitely grounded."

Genevieve nodded and gave her one more squeeze, then skipped away. Angie didn't even know where Harvey went.

When Angie reached her mom, Cooper was already being led away by his mom. He gave her one last look before reaching his own house next door. Angie's mom gave her a hard stare.

"What were you doing, Angie?" she asked.

"I thought that the neighbor was up to something," Angie mumbled.

Her mom sighed. "Well, did you find anything? Was it worth the two days you'll be grounded?"

Angie looked down. "Nothing. There was nothing in that room." She sighed and thought, *It's going to be a boring summer after all.*

CHAPTER 3

THE BIG IDEA

That night, Angie heard vehicles outside, and that strange buzzing sound came back. Angie could not figure out where it was coming from. So strange.

When she looked out the window, she saw a light glowing in the secret room and movement near the back door of Ms. Doody's house. Several people kept going in and out through the door.

She checked the time—three o'clock in the morning. This was definitely suspicious. Angie smiled to herself. Something was up after all.

After two long days of being grounded, Angie texted Cooper, Genevieve, and even Harvey to meet her at her house. They gathered in her yard, and Angie bounced on the balls of her feet.

"Ms. Doody"—they all giggled—"was up to something every single night while I was grounded. We have to get *into* that room," Angie said. She felt a pang of guilt. Her mom would be so mad at her. But if she was going to save the world, she couldn't worry about what her mom thought.

Cooper stared at her. Finally he said, "Are you kidding, Angie? There was nothing in there!"

Angie crossed her arms. "I think there is. We're just missing it somehow."

Cooper huffed. "You don't listen to anyone, Angie. I'm out of here," he said. Then he walked off.

Angie couldn't believe it. Cooper never abandoned her. Never. She sputtered for a moment, then took a deep breath, watching him walk away.

Genevieve gave her a sympathetic look. Harvey looked uncomfortable.

"There may be nothing in there, but I think we have to see for ourselves," Angie said. Without Cooper, though, she wasn't so sure.

Harvey said, "There was something in there, though. A laptop."

Angie blinked. Of course. If you wanted to take over the world, you'd probably plan it on a computer. She looked at Genevieve, who was already grinning. Genevieve was a whiz at computers.

"What's the plan?" Genevieve asked. Angie could have hugged her.

"Harvey, you ring the doorbell and distract Ms. Doody." After they all stopped giggling, she finished. "Get her away from the front door so we can slip in."

Harvey shifted on his feet. "Um . . . I'm not sure I'm the best person for this job. My mom says my social skills are one rung below a wolf child's."

Angie ignored him. "Let's go." She'd show Cooper she was right. She marched toward the house. Genevieve and Harvey had no choice but to follow her.

Angie and Genevieve hid by the side of the house, and Harvey rang the bell. When Ms. Doody answered, Harvey said, "Um, hi. I dropped my, uh . . . science experiment in your yard. Can you help me find it?"

Angie shook her head. Science experiment? But she heard Ms. Doody huff and watched as she walked away from the door with Harvey.

Ms. Doody complained loudly, "Children again! Today is a terrible day for this."

Angie and Genevieve snuck in. They got into the room with no problems, though the buzzing sound had gone away. Genevieve opened the laptop and got to work.

Angie leaned over the computer as Genevieve clicked around. Soon, she found a folder that said *World Domination Plan*. Genevieve clicked on it.

"Wow, she sure wasn't afraid of people getting into her computer," Genevieve whispered. The folder opened up.

Angie's breath caught in her throat. She had been right! Ms. Doody was planning on taking over the world.

And from what they found in the file, it seemed she was planning on doing it *today*.

Genevieve breathed out. She read, "Step one: Train insects. Check. Step two: Make growth serum. Check. Step three: Give serum to insects. Step four: Rule the world."

Angie saw a map of the room they were standing in. On it, an arrow pointed to the window they had tried to look in. Then there was a diagram of a secret drawer in the window frame on the inside. The serum, it seemed, was hidden in the woodwork around the window.

"It looks like the last two steps still haven't been done. Thank goodness. We need to steal the growth serum so she can't give it to the insects!" Angie said, her heart beating fast. "And then we gotta get out of here!"

But a voice from the doorway stopped her from moving.

"Not so fast, girlies." Ms. Doody pushed Harvey into the room with them. "Looks like I'll get to try out my plan on *three* foolish little children before it goes global."

CHAPTER 4

KICKING THE HORNET'S NEST

Ms. Doody stared at them.

"We know your plan," Angie said. She stepped in front of Genevieve and Harvey. "You are not going to get away with this!"

Ms. Doody laughed an evil laugh. "Oh yeah? Let's see what my babies have to say about this." She put two fingers in her mouth and whistled. With that, the buzzing sound came back.

Before Angie knew it, a swarm of insects flew to Ms. Doody and hovered around her head. There were wasps and hornets and other flying insects that looked terrifying. Angie shuddered, horrified.

"I don't need growth serum to take care of a few measly kids," Ms. Doody said. "I just have to whistle my attack whistle, and you all are toast. Any last words?" She grinned. "Wait, never mind. I don't care." Then she put her fingers in her mouth and took a deep breath. Angie squeezed her eyes shut and leaned into Genevieve and Harvey. She hadn't thought this would be her last day on earth. She was glad Cooper wasn't there—at least he would survive.

But just then, the doorbell rang.

Ms. Doody put her fingers down. "That must be my insect food. I have to feed my babies before they take over the world." She looked at Angie, Harvey, and Genevieve. "Not a sound, you hear?

If you are good, maybe I'll keep you around to do work for me. Get in that closet."

At first, Angie stood her ground.

Ms. Doody said, "I could have them attack you right now, you know." She put her fingers in her mouth again to whistle, but Angie put her hands up.

"Okay, okay!" she said. She, Harvey, and Genevieve crowded into the closet. Ms. Doody loomed large over them for a second, the insects still buzzing by her head.

"I'll deal with you later," she said and shut the door. Then she opened it again. "Wait. You probably have phones. Give them to me."

The doorbell rang again, and Ms. Doody huffed. "No one has any patience anymore." Angie reluctantly handed Ms. Doody her phone, and Genevieve and Harvey handed over theirs.

Genevieve said, "If I don't check in every hour, my mom comes looking for me. And you don't want my mom to find you."

Ms. Doody laughed. "Silly child. Your mom will have other things on her mind in an hour." Then she shut the closet door and turned the key in the lock.

They were stuck.

They heard Ms. Doody walk away, and Angie tried the door handle. It was no use. "I don't . . . have a plan," Angie said. Genevieve and Harvey were quiet. Angie felt close to tears. She was letting her friends down. Not to mention the world! Surely she could think of something. . . .

But before she could come up with anything, she heard some shuffling outside the closet. "Is she back already?" Genevieve whispered.

Angie steeled her shoulders. "When she opens

that door, let's all run at her. Maybe that will buy us some time."

Harvey and Genevieve nodded.

The key in the lock jiggled. Angie got ready to pounce. The door flung open, and the trio all roared and tumbled out of the closet at Ms. Doody. They landed in a pile on the floor.

Only it wasn't Ms. Doody. It was Cooper.

"Coop!" Angie yelled as they all climbed off of him.

Cooper said, "Shhh! We don't have much time." He groaned and got up. "We have to get out of here. I overheard everything she said. We need to tell your mom, Angie!"

"We need to get that serum," Angie said, walking to the window. She felt all around the edges.

"Angie!" Cooper said. "Come on!"

Harvey and Genevieve had already moved to the window and climbed out. Cooper climbed out too, then gestured frantically for Angie to hurry up.

Sweat had started to bead up on her forehead when she found a soft spot in the wood. She pushed it in, and a drawer slid out. In it sat a skinny tube filled with bright pink liquid. Angie grabbed it, but at the same time, the door to the room flung open.

Ms. Doody stood in the doorway, the light behind her bright, the bugs around her head buzzing angrily. She put her fingers to her lips, just as Angie threw one leg over the window ledge to climb out.

But it was too late. Ms. Doody whistled and yelled, "ATTACK!"

CHAPTER 5

TODDLER-
TASTROPHE

The insects swarmed at them, but Cooper slammed the window just as Angie got her leg out.

"RUN!" Angie yelled and took off. Harvey, Genevieve, and Cooper passed her pretty quickly—she wasn't the best runner. They took off through yards, jumping over bushes, rocks, fences, and anything else that got in their way.

Angie could hear the swarm of the angry

insects right behind her. She even felt one brush her ear, and she swatted it away.

But she was running out of steam. They needed a place to hide—and fast.

They ran all through the neighborhood toward the small center of their town.

Angie felt close to dropping. Her lungs burned, and she was starting to get a side ache.

Luckily, Cooper yelled, "This way!" and swerved into an alley.

The others followed him. To Angie's sheer joy, a door opened in one of the buildings along the alley. Cooper didn't even stop to explain to the surprised adult who had opened the door. He swept right past her, followed by Genevieve and Harvey.

Angie huffed her way to the door and saw the

adult's eyes widen as she caught a glimpse of the swarm of insects following close behind.

Angie raced in, and the adult closed the door one second before the insects followed.

"What the heck was that?" the adult said.

Angie bent down and put her hands on her knees, trying to catch her breath. She wasn't the only one. Cooper, Genevieve, and Harvey were also bent over and breathing hard.

The adult shook her head. "Well, I guess we won't take the kids out to the playground today," she said.

Angie stood up and looked around. They were in a large playroom that was empty. She heard yelling from little voices in a room next door.

"Where are we?" she said, still panting.

Cooper looked around too and then grinned. "We're at my sisters' day care! Hi, Mika!" he said to the adult.

She smiled at Cooper. "Hi, Cooper. I didn't recognize you in all the chase. So nice to see you. I bet Chloe and Cara would love to see you too."

"This is Mika," Cooper said to Angie, Genevieve, and Harvey. "She's the day care owner here. She watches my sisters."

Angie widened her eyes. "That's great, Coop. But we need to use the phone right now."

Cooper narrowed his eyes. "We have the serum, Angie. We're out of danger," he said quietly.

"I have to get back to the room," Mika said. "Come say hi to your sisters, Cooper!"

"We don't have time—" Angie said.

At the same time, Cooper said, "Yes!" He started walking to the door at the other end of the room.

Angie caught up with him. She held out the serum. "We have to get this someplace safe, Cooper!"

"We will," he whispered. "We can ask to use the phone once we're in here."

Angie huffed as they stepped into the room.

It was pure chaos. Toddlers ran around everywhere. Diapers were strewn all around the room. Toys cluttered every surface. Some kids were crying, some were laughing. Some fought in the corner and some just ran around in circles.

Cooper looked down at the serum and took it from Angie.

She tried to pull it back, but Cooper said, "Just

let me look at it." They wrestled with it back and forth, Genevieve and Harvey sharing a look.

"COOPER!" yelled two small voices through the din of all the other toddler noises. A tangled mess of braids and little kid arms and legs flew at them. Cooper and Angie were enveloped in big hugs from Chloe and Cara.

The twins pulled away and then ran back to the middle of the room. After she regained her balance, Angie watched as the twins stood close together with their backs to her. They were looking at something. Other toddlers began to crowd around them.

Angie looked down at her hands. She looked at Cooper's hands.

Their hands were empty.

Cooper and Angie looked at each other and said, "Oh no," at the same time.

Just then, Angie heard the sound of glass hitting the floor. A pink waft of serum enveloped the group of toddlers.

Angie watched in horror as the toddlers began to grow.

And grow . . . and grow . . . and grow . . .

Until their heads knocked into the ceiling and then pushed the ceiling clean off the building.

CHAPTER 6

DOODY DOODY EVERYWHERE AND NOT A SPOT TO STEP

The giant toddlers stepped out of the building.

Angie and Cooper stared at each other in horror. "Now what do we do?" Genevieve asked across the room.

At least ten toddlers were now as big as tall, tall buildings. They toddled off through the town. Angie, Cooper, Harvey, and Genevieve tried to follow them.

Cooper said, "I just hope my sisters don't—"

But then Angie saw what he was afraid of. Chloe and Cara looked at each other and giggled.

Then they unhitched their diapers and let them drop.

The four friends raced to get out of the way of the sloppy diapers, which were now as big as three buildings side by side. With a huge *THWUMP*, the diapers landed. To Angie's horror, poo spilled out of them and splatted on the buildings and on the street. She barely managed to jump out of the way of the splat.

Worse, the other toddlers saw the twins take off their diapers. One by one, each toddler unhitched their diapers.

Angie, Cooper, Genevieve, and Harvey started running. At each step, they were almost flattened

by gigantic soiled diapers. Just as they turned one way, another toddler was unhitching a diaper. As they ran away from that toddler, they ran toward another one who thought it was funny to drop his diaper.

THWUMP THWUMP THWUMP.

SPLATTTTT.

The town was now draped in dirty diapers. There was poo *everywhere*. Angie could barely breathe.

The toddlers started to play. They picked up cars and *vroooomed* them on the streets. One toddler grabbed a helicopter out of the sky and set it down right on top of one of the buildings.

But Chloe and Cara were the worst of the bunch. Each of them had poo in their hands, and they decided to throw it at each other and the other toddlers.

SPLAT.

SPLAT.

SPLATTTT.

The sound of the poo hitting things was almost as bad as the smell.

"Watch out!" yelled Cooper as a big pile of poo came tumbling down, almost on Angie's head. It didn't matter though. Anyone who was anywhere near the toddlers had poo all over them.

Adults lined the streets, yelling to the toddlers, "DO YOU WANT A TIME-OUT?" But the little ones weren't listening. One of the toddlers started to cry. Huge, deadly drops of tears began to land hard on the ground. Everyone on the street scattered.

Angie looked at her friends. "Now what?"

CHAPTER 7

GO 'GURT 'EM!

Genevieve said, "On the computer, I saw that there's an antidote in Ms. Doody's"—they all giggled a little—"house! It's under a floorboard below the window."

Angie said, "Well, that's something. Let's go! We can figure out what to do when we get there."

They ran as fast as they could back to their

neighborhood. They could hear the thumps of giant toddler feet behind them.

When they reached Ms. Doody's house, they found her sitting outside in her garden, her legs splayed out and her chin on her fist. A confused looking swarm of insects surrounded her. The four of them slowed down and tried to sneak past her. Right when they reached her door, she looked up.

"HEY! You kids ruined EVERYTHING! I hate children." She whistled, and the insects snapped into shape, swarming around her head. "Time for you to pay!"

She took a deep breath in to yell, but a big shadow blotted out the sun. She looked up and said, "What the heck?"

Chloe stood looking down at her, her face a little red and straining.

"Uh-oh, I know that look!" said Cooper. "Get inside!"

The four of them rushed into the house and shut the door. They heard a giant *SPLAT* and the windows got splattered with a huge pile of . . . poo.

Angie gagged. "I almost feel sorry for her!" she said.

"There's no time!" said Genevieve. While they'd watched Ms. Doody get splatted on, she'd run into the room and grabbed the antidote. "I have the cure. But how do we get it to the toddlers?"

They all looked at Angie expectantly. But she did something she never did. Maybe because she and Cooper had fought and gotten everyone in this mess. Or maybe because she remembered that Cooper was super smart and always had great ideas—whether she listened or not. Or maybe it was because she was covered in poo. But whatever the reason, she said, "Let's see if Cooper has any ideas."

Cooper smiled at her. He took a minute to think. Then his face lit up. "Yogurt! My mom had tons of it in our garage."

Angie whooped. "That's a perfect idea!" she yelled. She beamed at Cooper. "You know, sometimes you have some good things to say." Cooper smiled back at her.

Harvey said, "But how do we get them to eat it?"

Angie and Cooper looked at each other and grinned. "SQUIRT GUNS!" they said at the exact same time.

CHAPTER 8

MS. DOODY IS DONE

The four of them grabbed the squirt guns and filled them with Cooper's mom's yogurt. Angie tasted it just to be sure. It really was delicious. They added drops of the antidote to each squirt gun.

Then they ran outside and squirted their first toddler—Chloe. She licked her lips and instantly shrunk down to her normal toddler size. She immediately started crying.

Cooper's mom came out of her house and grabbed Chloe. She saw Cooper and said, "What is going on?" Then she plugged her nose.

Cooper yelled, "Be back in a sec, Mom!"

Angie yelled, "Your yogurt is delicious, Ms. Sanchez!"

Then the four of them sprinted to the town, dodging doody and other unpleasant things, to shoot some toddlers with yogurt.

One by one, each toddler shrank down to toddler size. Adults grabbed the toddlers as they went back to normal. Soon, the day care was filled with crying, dirty, smelly, tired toddlers.

Angie, Cooper, Genevieve, and Harvey walked back to Angie's house. They had doody smeared everywhere, and Angie had never been so tired in her life. But she felt great.

Not only had they saved the world, but the summer *definitely* wasn't boring so far.

When they got back to Angie's house, they saw Ms. Doody—covered in poo—loading up her car.

"YOU AGAIN!" she yelled. "My babies are gone, and now I have nothing! But no matter, I'll just try again in the next town."

Angie sighed. Really, she was too tired for this. "Do you guys have any ideas on how to stop her?"

Cooper grinned. "I like this new thing of you listening to other people."

Angie grinned back.

Just then, a siren sounded near them. Angie's mom pulled up in her sheriff's car. "Ms. Doody," she said—the kids all giggled. Angie thought her mom might have even snickered a little. "You are under arrest! Put your hands up."

Angie was thrilled. "Mom! How did you know she was behind this?"

As her mom put handcuffs on Ms. Doody, she said, "You know I *do* listen to you. I talked to Mika at the day care, and I figured Ms. Doody"—everyone giggled, Angie's mom included—"was behind this. You're my daughter—your instincts are pretty good," she said and smiled.

As she closed Ms. Doody in the backseat, she walked to the driver's side door. "Oh, and Cooper, good news! The day care decided to pick up your mom's yogurt. It really is delicious." She shut her door and said, "All right, Angie, I'll see you later tonight. I have some cleaning up to do." She turned on the sirens and drove away.

Ms. Doody glared at all four of them for as long as she could before the car disappeared down the street.

Cooper threw his arm around Angie and she threw her arm around Genevieve, who threw her arm around Harvey.

"Well, that was an interesting start to our summer," Cooper said.

Angie smiled. "I can't wait to see what else happens! Didn't you think that day care seemed haunted or something? We should probably do some investigating. . . ."

All of them groaned, but Angie couldn't stop smiling.

GLOSSARY

antidote (AN-ti-dote)—a medicine to cure a poison

bellow (BELL-oh)—to yell very loudly

circumstances (SUR-kuhm-stan-sez)—facts or conditions that are connected to an event

deputy (DEP-yoo-tee)—a person, often in law enforcement, who reports to a boss, normally a sheriff

drawl (DRAWL)—to speak in a slow manner

gleefully (GLEE-fuhl-ee)—in a very joyful manner

proactive (proh-AK-tiv)—to make something happen instead of reacting to something

serum (SEER-uhm)—a liquid that is used to prevent or cure a disease

sympathetic (sim-puh-THET-ik)—expressing feelings of pity or sadness for someone else who's going through something hard

toddle (TAWD-uhl)—to move with short, unsteady steps

trespass (TRES-pas)—to go onto someone's property without permission

DISCUSSION QUESTIONS

1. How did Angie change over the course of the story? How did she stay the same?

2. Throughout the book, Cooper seems frustrated about Angie not listening to him. If you had a friend like Angie, how would you let her know that you want her to listen to you?

3. If Angie and her friends hadn't found an antidote, what else do you think the toddlers might have gotten up to?

WRITING PROMPTS

1. What investigation do you think Angie and her friends will take on next? Write your own funny story about the friends' next adventure.

2. Imagine you're a news reporter in Angie's town. Write an article about what happened with Ms. Doody, the toddlers, and Angie and friends.

3. What was Ms. Doody thinking when she planned to unleash giant insects in her neighborhood? Write a paragraph or two from her perspective. How does she feel about her plans being ruined by the neighborhood kids?

ABOUT THE AUTHOR

MEGAN ATWOOD is a writer and professor with more than 45 books published. She lives in New Jersey, where she wrangles cats, dreams up ridiculous stories, and thinks of ways to make kids laugh all day.

ABOUT THE ILLUSTRATOR

ETHEN BEAVERS lives in Central California and has been working in children's books, comics, and animation for more than ten years. He is a big fan of Star Wars and Samurai Jack, as well as fly-fishing for trout across the western U.S.

JOKING AROUND

How do you get a baby astronaut to sleep?
You rocket!

Why did the coach hire a baby for his team?
Because it's so good at dribbling!

What did the baby computer call his father?
Data!

Why did the cowboy give cough syrup to the pony?
It was a little hoarse!

What did the hamburger name its baby?
Patty!

What do they call babies in the army?
Infantry!

What do you get if you cross a baby with a mountain?
A cry for Alp!

What do you find on the bottom of a baby cloud?
Thunderwear!